Polythrenody

First Edition
March 2021

Polythrenody

POLYTHRENODY
An Anthology

NICK ARCHER

Polythrenody

Polythrenody

CONTENTS

YELLOW AFTER DARK

It's still raining when Candice looks to see James staring in the window of the diner, which to all intents and purposes, is a greasy spoon cafe but for the fact that it does not lock its door.

Drenched in neon reds and greens, it serves coffee and home-made pie and offers respite from the darkness of the world beyond those plate-glass windows.

Spattered with droplets, James stares in through them from the night side; he is soaked with rain and drenched in shadow.

The sight of him makes Candice's stomach tighten.

He's here; it's time.

I stare in through the window, my breath fogging the glass. Inside I can see shapes, vaguely human, barely moving. They are lit by the glow of humming colour around the diner. Their faces are hidden; I need to go inside.

The warm air is stale and rushes at me when I push the door open. It creaks on its hinge. The sound makes three heads swivel to look at me, and I meet their gazes.

One of them knows.

I approach the counter, a long strip of metal and plastic at the far end. The man behind it is tall and broad, like me.

Sat on a stool on this side is an older man, withered and hunched, a khaki anorak draped over his narrows shoulders like a thrift-store wraith. His sunken eyes glare at me as I stand beside him, but I ignore them.

I assume the man behind the counters is Dan; the moniker is scrawled in cheap neon above his head.

'Evening. Coffee?'

'Information.'

My bluntness doesn't seem to bother him. It's like he's been expecting it.

'We do coffee here, and cake. Nothing else.'

I feel rattled, sensing that scrunching up of my

stomach, the clenching of my fist in my pocket.

Breath in.

'I'm looking for my son.'

Breath out.

Dan's expression doesn't change, but I feel the old man tense beside me. I glance at him. He is staring up at me through wiry eyebrows; cold eyes, dark with judgement.

I continue, 'I was told he was here.'

It is the old man who replies, 'Well he's not.'

Dan's hand shoot across, holds his palm out to calm him, 'Easy, Terry.' His tone is firm but gentle. The old man's prickles relax into his anorak.

To me, Dan says, 'Look around. It's not a big place. You can see he's not here.'

I scan the room slowly. There is only a young woman, her back to me.

No sign of my son, and yet I have a sense that I cannot leave.

Not yet.

'Tea', I demand, 'Camomile.'

With my hot mug warming my palm, I cross the diner and slide into one of the plastic bucket seats. I set the mug down on the cracked Formica tabletop and bow my head, pressing my hands into my eyes until all I see are flickering spots.

He's here. I know he's here.

I release my face, dropping my hands to the mug, cupping it and see movement ahead of me.

Two tables away, a little diecast toy car is placed on the surface. The tiny hand that deposited it disappears below, only to return with a second car that parks behind the first. A third is butted up behind them both.

I watch with tired eyes as the hand pops up a fourth time, but this time a tiny yellow flower is carefully laid down at the end of the train.

I'm suddenly aware of my heart pounding in my head and shake it until it stops.

I look at Dan and Terry, and they are pretending not the look at me.

The door creaks and clatters and someone new walks in. A young man, a hoodie pulled down as he stalks across the diner to the counter, meeting my eye as he passes. I do not look away, waiting for him to, but not until he scowls. Aggression radiates from him in waves.

He turns away to order coffee and my view of him is blocked.

Polythrenody

A young woman sits in front of me. She is petite in her frame, but her shoulders are broad, her arms long; they fold across her yellow top, and her head tilts a little as she smiles.

'Are you okay?' Her hair is long, straight, she moves it with an air of nervousness.

I want to be annoyed at her intrusion, but somehow, I am not. Still, I answer gruffly, 'No.'

'I'm sorry to hear that,' she says, then adds, 'I'm Candice.'

I shrug and sip my tea. It has already gone cold. I can feel her watching me, so I ask, 'What do you want?'

Candice pauses, considering her words, 'I knew your son.'

I frown, lean forward, 'Here?'

'Once. But not for a while now. He's not here any more.'

I grunt, 'You're lying. Here's here.'

Her expression is insistent, 'No, I'm not. I liked Chris. He was always very kind to me, but at the same time, he seemed very lost.

'Did you ever get that feeling?'

I look down at my mug, 'I knew that he was hurting, but he'd never tell me why. Or couldn't. Words just seemed to get stuck in the air between us.'

As I speak, the young man in the hoodie is taking his coffee to a stool further along the counter, moving into my line of sight. I catch his eye again, refuse to release it and I see his jaw clench.

'I know the feeling,' Candice says, drawing my attention back to her.

'You were friends?', I ask.

She half nods, and I reply to the motion, 'I can see him liking you. You would be his type.'

Candice laugh, suddenly and loudly. All eyes dart to her, to me. She chuckles, 'I'm not so sure that's accurate.'

'No, he liked gentle people. He's a gentle boy... quiet... delicate.'

My mind drifts back in time, to my son, playing with his cars in the park. He would leave them there, I'd recall, almost every time, he'd forget them. And other boys, they wouldn't play with him. Else they'd taunt him, make him cry.

'What are you staring at?'

The voice startles me. I am looking at the young man as I come back to the present. He stares at me, without blinking, the promise of violence in his tone.

Why is he reacting so readily? Defensively.

Because he knows something.

I am on my feet quickly, my hand catching my mug and tipping it over. Candice jumps. I sense movement from the others, but I am a locomotive, barrelling towards another.

Dan is between us, having jumped the counter, trying to defuse and placate, but my mouth is running and what I am saying I cannot even understand myself.

The young man is shouting at me, at Dan, 'I didn't start this! This old boy needs to back off before -'

I don't hear the rest, because Terry is now weighing in, pulling on Dan's clothes, trying to let the young man get at me, 'Let him do it, Dan! He bloody deserves it after all he's done!'

They're all hiding something, I realised with bitter clarity and grab at Terry's anorak, 'Tell me where my son is!'

'I ain't telling you anything!'

Dan attention is split between three separate alterations; at first two involving me, but a stray word from Terry creates friction with the young man and suddenly they are calling each other names.

I step back a little and catch sight of something.

There is a little corridor beside the counter, and at its mouth, just for a moment, is a little boy. His pure face is illuminated for a moment, then he is gone.

I move quickly after him. The corridor dark and empty but for a glow coming from the open one of two doors.

When I get to the doorway, I find a stainless steel kitchen. The worktops are scratched and dulled from use, but still manage to reflect the sodium light streaming from security lights outside the high, narrow windows.

At the far end stands the boy.

My eyes sting. I rub them again, my vision blurred. staring back at me and my throat closes up, 'Chris?'

He speaks, and although my ears are ringing, I can hear him, 'When I was small, we were so close, dad. You and I on our adventures. It didn't matter if we were shopping or playing in the park. We were a team; we would always be a team, you said.

'But I got older, I got lost. It wasn't your fault, and it wasn't mine. Black and white became grey, everything that we took for granted was no longer there, and even the most simple things became complex.'

I step forward, squinting, trying to make sense of the words, the source of them unclear, confusing.

'I became lost in a darkness I did not understand, and neither did you. We lost each other there. Our team was broken.'

I feel a hand on my cheek. It is soft. Familiar.

'It took many, difficult years, but I found my way out of the dark. I discovered, and became, who I always was, but to you, I was changed.'

The small boy leans forward, comes into focus and Candice says softly, 'I knew you loved me, but it wasn't enough. I don't know what caused it, but you couldn't follow me out of the dark; your mind wouldn't let you.'

My mind feels suddenly lighter. The words fall from my mouth as I touch the face of the child that I had never lost, 'Candice.'

It's still raining when Candice looks to see James staring back at them at the door of the late-night diner. He is smiling at her. He knows their face. They can feel love for them.

Dan is beside them, his hand on their shoulder as he frowns with concern, 'This has got to stop, Candice. People got hurt this time.'

Candice nods sadly, 'I know, Dan. I do. All I can do is thank you all, but I think we're getting closer.'

Both look at Terry bandaging his hand.

Dan sighs, 'We'll help you all he can, but we might be

right back here in a few months if his mind doesn't accept - '

'I know', Candice interrupts him, placing a hand on his, 'But I have to believe that it will, Dan. I have to hope, because what else is there?'

Without another word, Dan steps away, returns to his counter.

From the street, James smiles at Candice and they smile back. They watch their father leave the diner once more.

DELUGE

Neil

When the ceiling breaks, it cracks like thunder, a sudden and deafening sound that sends tremors through the living room.

You hear it fall.

Hear the paper that covers the surface rip, the wet wood twist and sheer, the plaster crash into the desk where you were sat just seconds before.

You don't see it. Your back is to the place where your computer sits with your paperwork and your diaries and your textbooks,

After the initial, ear-rending cacophony, the noise fades, like someone slowly turning the volume down. Chunks of plaster and wood and other things still fall, for a moment, slow, then stop completely.

Polythrenody

A tap twisted shut.

Then it is quiet. Only the relentless hammering of the rain outside the window, that until only a few moments ago you were enjoying the music of.

An elemental symphony, exquisite in its random sonata, it's repetitive chords comforting, knowing that it is beyond wall and window. You are safe in your manufactured cave.

Nature may scream and howl at your door, but inside, you are quietly victorious against her.

The forecast had boldly proclaimed a light shower, but it seemed the rival forces of high and low pressure had other plans for you.

Yet now, you feel smaller particles, errant debris charting their own, separate path to the group, hitting the top of your abundant yet greying hair.

You dare not turn around at first.

At this moment you are free of the truth your eye will provide, existing in a comfortable state of sensory ignorance, almost ambivalence.

You *heard* it, and you *felt* it, but you didn't *see* it.

It might not be what you think.

You have always been known for your ample imagination; this is just another example of that.

Then the smell hits you.

Polythrenody

Dank and musty, the pervasive odour of moisture, the unmistakable child of wood and water together.

You turn your head and see the chaos. Chunks of plaster and shards of wood and islands of torn paper, all covering your large expensive desk. The twin flat-screen monitors are covered in white and grey dust, the keyboard lost beneath a strip of sodden paper, the once elegant tower battered by what remains of wooden boards.

And water.

Dear God, the water.

There is so much of it.

Nature has defied your arrogance and insisted upon behind let in. Here it laughs at you, a torrent of water pouring inside like a south American waterfall, splashing across the ornate desk and into the plunge pool once called the carpet.

In seconds, there I half an inch of water around your slippers.

You look at the technology, destroyed beyond repair and the piles of test papers that you were marking, saturated and now a single block of papier-mache.

Annihilated.

Gone.

And you smile.

Here, you think, is an opportunity.

Susan

You are shoving your bras into the gap between your blouses and skirts in the large suitcase when you hear it.

The whole bungalow seems to shudder, twice, like a shiver running through its body. The first is a crack and thud and the second seems more like a sigh.

It makes you jump and your heart suddenly starts pounding, your mind is alert, adrenaline flooding your veins.

Your body is preparing you.

Fight or flee.

The thought amuses you; you were already fleeing.

Taking your hand from the suitcase you step into the middle of the bedroom, listening.

The rain is still blasting down on the roof above, making it hard to hear anything else, but you can just about make out a new sound.

It is like a window has been left open, and the sound of pouring water is no longer muted behind glass panes, but clear and present.

You wipe tears of anger from your eyes, pushing your

glasses up to access them, sniff to clear your nose and in turn, your mind.

You want to call out to Neil, but his name is still bitter in your mouth, and just listen for him instead. A few seconds pass and he does not call your name either.

What on earth has just happened?

In your gut, you know, what you don't want to surmise, just in case you are correct.

Why isn't he calling out to you? Why isn't he coming running in?

You look at the suitcase on the bed, at the clothes still stacked high in it. Far too many to close the lid on, and your hoes are not yet in it, or your toiletries, or any of the myriad items that define your settled life.

How does one condense twenty years into one suitcase? Everything little thing you are forced to leave behind seems to be a part of you, no matter how trivial you once considered it to be.

Every bit of plastic and wood and paper has a history, is drenched with memories.

Damn him.

It was perfect and Neil had gone and made a mess of everything.

You sigh, long and furious with frustration in every ounce of air expelled through pursed lips, and know that you need to go and see what has happened.

You leave the bedroom, walk along the wide corridor, past the photo of you and Neil is Morocco and Uruguay and Hong Kong and New Zealand, and all the flea-market paraphernalia you bought together along the way.

You come to the doorway of the living room, but stay back, just out of sight and look at your husband.

He is tall and still handsome in his 50s, grey and chiselled and even his gathering crows feet add only to his charm, and it makes you hate him all the more.

He stands in the room, slowly turning to see his beloved desk, crushed beneath the remains of the ceiling above it. You see that he has an empty cup of tea in his hand; he must have only just stood up to make a fresh one when the world caved in behind him.

A flicker of relief then, that he had moved, just in time. Less than a second later, and he would have been in the same sorry state as the desk.

You watch in regret as he stares at it, then your eyes widen and you see what he does next, and your mouth drops open.

Neil glances back at the door, and you step out of sight to watch.

Neil

You drop the cup on the floor and hear it break, risking a quick look at the living room door.

Susan has not come in yet. You still have time.

No, this is stupid. Only a fool would consider something like this.

Someone desperate.

You raise an eyebrow at your inner self.

You *are* desperate.

Rainwater pours in, the broken panels above splitting the torrent into five or six waterfalls that crash into the desk and the carpet and the leather swivel chair.

Do it, you think, before you change your mind, before your inner coward wins out.

You take three or four quick, deep breaths and put your head under the crashing spouts, instantly soaking your hair and your shirt. The sudden coldness takes your breath away, but you keep going.

The noise is all around you now as you sit in the chair, the water filling he indentation like a child paddling pool and you immerse your backside in it.

It feels ridiculous, but you keep going. You pick the shreds of paper and plastic up and cover yourself in it, draping it across you, rubbing wet dust, now almost paste, into your cheeks and hair.

How has it come to this, you ask yourself, this final desperate act of insanity to save your dying marriage?

It should only have been a fling, you have reflected much in the last few hours; you should have stopped it months ago.

But you couldn't. You were addicted. Addicted to being wanted. The desire for desire was the most powerful drug you had ever known and Jenny was both dealer and substance.

Susan had found out, only hours ago and they had argued since he had come in from work. An age of exhausting, unanswerable questions and denials and admissions and apologies and deflections.

The result had been her throwing her clothes into a suitcase, ready to go to her sisters, whilst you had sat at his desk to mark test papers to show that you did not care.

But you did. You cared very much.

And you sit now, filled with regret and remorse and covering yourself with the fetid flesh of your home, one last Hail Mary to rescue your marriage.

It's not enough, you say to yourself, not nearly enough.

Your head dizzy with the cold of the water, your heart

pounding with the intensity of your resolve, you do
what needs to be done, suddenly and brutally.

Susan

You press your manicured fingernails against your
nose as you watch the man you had spent twenty years
of your life with, stage the scene to win you over.

To win you back.

He's an idiot.

But then he always was, and tonight has simply
proven that point beyond all reasonable doubt.

Dripping wet and covered with the tattered entrails of
the home you have paid for together for half a decade,
sitting in the chair and already looking forlorn and
beaten, you watch in awe as he goes one step further.

It is so sudden you wonder if it really happened. Neil
grips the edge of the desk, and brings his face down so
hard and so fast you literally jump at the sound of the
impact.

You cover your hand with your mouth, almost feel the
pain as if it were your nose that had just been broken
on the wood.

You watch Neil do it a second time, the sheer,

masochistic violence of it making you gasp allowed this time.

Behind the veil of splashing water, he cannot hear you. You step forward a little, peer through at Neil as he peels his broken face away from the edge of the desk. Facing away, you cannot see what damage there is, but you can see the drops of crimson now staining the pooling water on the carpet.

What a fool he is. This was all so unnecessary. A poorly conceived comment, innocent in its intention, and almost trivial to boot, but it had unravelled Neil's lies.

You feel frustration rise in your chest. You are no fool, unlike your husband.

You had known about the existence of Jenny for months, her presence in the periphery of your life and you had not just accepted it, but you had welcomed it.

Guilt is a wonderful gift to the contrivance of romance, it makes the mind sharper, makes the guilt party more attentive. In the past six months, you had enjoyed gifts and holidays and small acts of thoughtfulness that you never knew that Neil was capable of.

Since Easter, your marriage had been in the best shape since their first two years, before he took on more responsibility at the university, and you, the role of Senior Project Manager at your firm.

It was unplanned, but it had created an opportunity that you had taken advantage of.

You had not looked for Brian, but he had appeared at just the right moment. Younger than you, though not as young as Neil's "mature" 28-year-old student, Brian had made her feel alive again.

You smile. It was Neil who had saved their marriage, all the while fearing that he was endangering it with his infidelity.

There would be those who would cynically judge what their relationship had become, but you and Neil had built a life together; a home, domestic habits, holidays, plans for a second home in France.

You still want these things.

You desire ownership of your cake, and you want it consumed.

And you had it all, until Neil, the idiot, had threatened it all.

You have ignored so much, overlooked his obvious lies, his pathetic attempts at deceit. One comment, made by him, so utterly absurd that he knew that he had caught himself out.

He said nothing, but his eyes had confessed.

And you could ignore it no longer, for to so would have made you out to be a fool yourself.

You could not have this. You had no choice but to react and he had confessed it all, and what he took at anger at his unfaithfulness, was in fact fury at him ruining what you had.

In twenty years, you had never been so wrathful of him.

But now, as you watch him, soaked and battered and bloody, his spirit broken, you feel affection for him.

Your heart flutters.

He's trying.

You will try too, and if you play this right, within weeks he'll be throwing himself at Jenny again, and you can continue with Brian, guilt-free.

Neil

Your face burns as though you had just buried in a pit of fire. Having never been in a real fight, your face has remained a virgin territory for physical violence. This sudden trauma is more shocking than you ever considered that it might be.

Pushing yourself away from the desk seeing your

blood running in tiny rivulets, mixing with the water, becoming one with it, you wonder if you had dreamed this incident; that this is some lucid exploration of your subconscious, your guilt rising to the surface like bubbles and popping.

You had worried before if you could carry off this farce, having never excelled in acting, but shivering with the cold and wet, your face cracked and bleeding and aching, no performance is required.

Behind you, you hear feet splashing through the sodden carpet and then a warm, firm hand on your back, your shoulders your neck. You are turned, the debris is brushed from you, soft hands are on your cheeks, delicate fingers touch your broken nose.

You look up at Susan, her eyes full of concern, of worry and sympathy; emotions you have not elicited in her for many years and you feel tears prickled your eyes.

Real tears.

You reach out to her, grab onto her and she lifts you, away from the chair and the desk, the Broadway stage of your ruse.

Susan embraces you, asks if you're okay and if you're hurt anywhere else. You don't answer, just embrace her, bury your face in her neck and her hair and live in that moment every moment since you met her.

You are a fool, you realise. Jenny only made you feel young, wanted, and looked up to, but it was all false.

Like this desperate act of deceit here, that relationship was all phoney.

This, right here, *this* woman, is real as the water pouring in over them.

You hold her tight and make a promise to yourself, that you would remain faithful to Susan forevermore. You'd make her happy again.

You hold her tighter, feel her respond in kind.

As you do, you look out of the window, and not for the first time wonder how wrong the weather forecast had been.

CAFÉ DEXTER

There is a place further up the street, but it is cold and wet, and I am tired. My choice of attire today has been found lacking. Mistakes have been made. My waterproof coat is hanging up by the door at home, having been usurped by the far warmer fleece-lined, cord bomber jacket with the fluffy collar.

It has been snowing since the day before, so logic would dictate that it was the correct choice, but as the day had gone on, the flakes had become considerably wetter.

As a result, my jacket and woolly gloves are soaked through, and even my feet are beginning to hurt.

It's strange how something can appear in one way, yet be revealed to be another.

I step through the doorway, feeling that first rush of warm air from within the cafe envelope me. I shouldn't be here, but I need to get out of the billowing flakes that soak like rain.

The cafe is almost entirely full of people huddling to escape the weather. A few heads turn automatically as I enter, scan me swiftly then return to their own conversations, or staring into their hot coffee like a hobo might a barrel of flames.

I shuffle between a pair of parked pushchairs, offering a cursory apology under my breath. There are no tables free, but there are a few stools still vacant at the long counter and I swiftly pick the nearest one.

It's silly, but I feel more comfortable closer to the door. Groaning, I release the four shopping bags from my grasp, letting them slide slowly to the tiled floor. Their handles pulled taught with the weight of the cargo beneath have etched deep, painful grooves into my fingers. I extend and ball them into a fist, trying to encourage the circulation to return, having been driven away by cold and pressure.

I must hiss through my teeth louder than I thought because I feel someone looking at me from further down the counter.

Bright, blue eyes, wide and amused. She smiles knowingly at my pain. I can see a pile of shopping bags by her feet too. We share a moment of shared misery at the blight of annual festive consumerism, but she holds my gaze a little longer than simple mutual acknowledgement.

She is pretty. Blonde, seemingly short from the fact that her feet are nowhere near the ground on the stool, and curvy. Her stylish red Parka is unbuttoned at the front in an effort to cool her down, and she is what my mother would have called buxom.

I look away, not wanting to push my luck. I'll play it cool, order my coffee, then try to catch her eye again a few moments. If I can, I might break the habit of a lifetime and shuffle clumsily down the counter to talk to her.

At twenty-two, I had only ever had two girlfriends, one a summer fling, the other lasting three years. Having been single for nearly eighteen months, I am more than ready to get back on that particular horse.

The person behind the counter is a tall, slim black man with a shaved head and pointed features, serving alongside a tiny woman in her sixties with dark curly hair. She has an archetypal gipsy quality, her fingers are heavy with garish rings. I raise my head and the man notices me.

'Coffee, please,' I say, then have to repeat it over the noise of the cafe. He juts his chin, grabs a pot and cup, starts to pour it. As he does, I notice a neat sign printed on plastic above the counter.

RIGHTS ONLY.

In the past, such a notice would have bothered me more, but these days I am as comfortable as I can be in places like this. As I said, there was a more welcoming place at the other end of the block, but for the sake of a quick coffee and five minutes to thaw, it's worth the risk.

Now filled to the brim, I ensure to take the up coffee with my right hand, deftly bringing it to my lips with practised ease.

The man steps away to serve the next person, a refill on their coffee and I glance at the girl again.

This time she is not looking at me. Instead, she is pressing the screen of her phone with cold, clumsy fingers. There are used plates in front of her; a large one containing the remnants of a panini, half a chocolate fudge cake on the smaller. The cutlery is placed casually on the right-hand edge of both.

Suddenly, she finishes thumbing her phone and raises her head to catch the attention of the servers. It is the woman who attends to her. I can't hear their voices, but the girl clearly wants to pay, and as she speaks, her gaze drifts across to me.

It lingers on me, even as she speaks to the woman.

I smile to myself.

Game on.

She clearly on the verge of leaving, so I'll have to move fast. Either that or I finish my coffee quickly to coincide with her departure, catch her as she steps out onto the street.

I frown into my cup. It's risky; could come off as stalker-like, and it is damned cold out there. I was hoping to push my luck in here for at least ten minutes before venturing back out into the elements.

I glance over. She is wrapping her scarf around her neck, shaking her hair out.

Our gazes meet again, for a moment.

Damn, she *is* cute. If I don't give it a go, I'll be kicking myself all weekend.

Screw it. Go for it. The worst outcome is she gives me a disgusted look and walks away. The best-case scenario is that I might have a buddy to keep me warm over New Years.

The woman approaches the girl and passes the bill over, and the girl takes it.

My heart leaps a little. My stomach sinks.

She had taken it in her right hand, the same as every other person in here but me, but in a moment of pure instinct, her left hand had twitched first.

I look around quickly. No one else had noticed it, and she has recovered expertly. Still, it was almost a mistake that she should not have made.

She pays with cash, this time making the exchange using her right hand where appropriate and stands, gathering her shopping bags. As she stands, she looks at me again.

It's so on, I think.

I'll wait until she almost at the door, then down my coffee and set off in pursuit. With any luck, my bravery will hold out until I can catch up with her on the street; there I'll see if she wants to grab another coffee in the other place.

A cafe that we'll both be more comfortable in. A place that we can be ourselves.

I sip my coffee. It's not cooling down very fast. I'll have to leave most of it.

Getting ready, I wrap my fingers around the handles of the bag and watch her stand. She starts easing her way through the crowded floor, between the tables, strays legs and bags.

At the far side, there is another pushchair and a baby on a woman's knee. As the girl passes, the baby throws its dummy on the floor by her feet. My heart leaps into my throat as she stops, allows the bags to rest on the door. The straps go limp as she reaches down to pick the dummy up.

I watch, numb, as she hands it back to the mother whose eyes are suddenly aflame with disgust and indignity. The mother's mouth drops open and she leans away, pulling her baby away from the dummy proffered in the girl left hand.

'Dirty fucking leftie!'

The girl looks at her own hand, and almost in shock at the sight of it, realises her mistake. She shakes her head, swaps it to her right, but it is too late.

On the table behind the mother, two men with white beards and deeply wrinkled brows snap their heads at the words, their eyes cutting into the girl.

She shakes her head, then smiles and frowns all at once, saying, 'No, I'm not. It's just my other hand is full of bags.'

Then three pairs of eyes are looking at her hands, to where her cargo is split equally between her limbs.

The lie is laid bare, and the girl knows it. My heart is pounding and I feel suddenly hot in the stuffy space.

Run, I scream at her with my mind, *go now!*

It's like she hears me. She steps past the mother, hurrying towards the door but the second of the older men steps across her path.

She smiles nervously, 'I'm not leftie… I'm just in a hurry.'

Then a voice is bellowing over my shoulder, the man from the counter, 'What the hell's going on?'

The second older man replies, self-righteous anger burnt into his tone, 'You've got a leftie in here, pal!'

'What? Who?' The server is craning his thin neck, trying to see through the heads. All the heads in the cafe are now turned towards the girl. All conversation has now stopped. The stifling air is now thick with silence.

I watch the girl swallows, her voice trembling, 'I'm not leftie… please, I'm not.'

It's an Asian woman who speaks next, almost spitting, 'Write your name then! Prove it.'

As if in answer, a pen in thrust forward, held aloft amidst the rumble of talk about the girl.

I am frozen. My finger wrapped around the bags, almost too afraid to move unless I too am uncovered.

The girl looks at the pen, blinking sweat from her eyes, then carefully takes it.

Another person slides a scrap of paper, perhaps a bill or receipt, over to her. Her hand shaking, the girl leaves the shopping bags on the floor and moves to the table with the paper.

The pen, quivering in her grip, lowers to the paper. The nib presses against the rough surface but doesn't move.

'Go on then. Nothing to worry about unless you're lying to us.'

I watch her close her eyes, tears form in the corners and she mutters, 'I just wanted coffee… it's cold outside.'

A raucous, emphatic cheer rises from the room; the joy of discovering the liar, their own worth now elevated by it.

'Can't you read?', the serving-man says, 'Rights Only. There's a place for your kind further down the street.'

The girl looks down, 'I'm sorry, I'm leaving.' She looks for her bags, realises that she still has the dummy in her left hand and turns to the mother.

Cautiously, she holds it out to her, and the mother looks like she might actually vomit. She spits acidly, 'I don't want that thing now you've had your filthy leftie hands on it! How dare you even think of giving it to my child! You're disgusting!'

The strike is sudden and startling. Open palm across the girls face. The dummy drops to the floor. There are groans from those appalled at the violence, muted cheers from those pleased by justice being done.

'Got to learn their lesson.'

'Disgusting attitude, they have.'

'Can't just come in here like that, it's not right.'

Those who were quieter before are becoming more vocal. Some cannot look away. Others want to see how it will turn out. A few are leaving, and it is these who concern me. They are going before it escalates; perhaps they don't fully agree with the status quo, but they are too afraid to stand against it.

I much as I hate to admit it, I understand that.

I sit, rooted to the spot, a fraud amongst the Rights, saying nothing through fear that I might be next.

I am as ashamed as I am terrified.

Then it gets worse.

The girl responds to the mother in kind. Her own slap is equal in both force and surprise, yet whereas the mother took pride in hers, the girl immediately understands what she has done.

It was instinct. It was a burst of anger and frustration, born out of years of persecution and oppression the like of which the mother had never, and would never, know or understand.

Human, no, animal nature; to push back, when pushed too far.

Rationality, however, and the realisation of consequence, is a bucket of cold water to the girl.

Polythrenody

It is the older men who grab her, pulling her across the table, and the Asian woman is grabbing her too. People are moving, standing up to see or to get involved.

I lose sight of her.

My heart is hammering outside of my chest. I want to run. I don't want to see it. I want to help. I know I can't

It shouldn't be like this. She should be outside, getting wet in the sleet, listening to me clumsily chat her up. She should be politely rejecting me right now, or we should we walking to the Left-Friendly cafe exchanging shy conversation.

Instead, I am smothered by the shame of my fear, watching her being pulled apart by a mob driven by hate.

There is a scream and I sense the crowd parting a little. Through the heads, I can discern the girl standing up, stumbling backwards. Her hair is in disarray and there is a sizeable fresh bruise on her cheek, a cut on her lip and eyebrow.

They are shouting at her, calling her a thug. Someone else if saying that she had stabbed them, and I can glimpse the pen in her hand. The blue plastic is now red with blood.

'Call the police!' Another shouts, making my blood run

cold.

When the police become involved in these situations, I have come to learn in my life, things tend to escalate out of all proportion. There is an institutional fear, seemingly trained into them by their forebears. Where it stems from, I have never been able to fully understand, but it prompts swift and inexplicably violent action. I have seen on the news, and I have witnessed it first hand on two occasions. Both times, I have been left with an inescapable sense that, being simply who I was born to be, I was living on borrowed time.

The girl is backed into the corner, wide-eyed and terrified. This was the person I simply wanted to talk to, to have a drink with, perhaps date.

Now, this is all impossible. It might as well have never happened at all.

I should have continued on to the cafe at the end of the block. This incident, with the girl, would still have occurred, but at least I would not have had to have seen it. I could have lived in blissful ignorance, at least until it was *me* who made the mistake; until it was, finally and inevitably, me in that corner, holding a blood-drenched biro.

I have to go. I've stayed too long.

Leaving the bags on the floor, I stand and push my way to the door, trying to ignore the venomous shouting and taunting directed at the girl, and her racking sobs of despair and self-pity.

As I reach the door, people running towards it, and at the last moment, I realise that they are the police; told that there is a 'violent leftie' inside.

I grab the door and yank it open, allowing them to charge past before I dart out into the snow. As I pass them, one catches my eye. His gaze is filled with predetermined judgement, and although I try not to meet it, I feel it burning into me.

I let go of the handle and realise, that in my primal haste to leave, I have made my own mistake.

The door handle falls away from the release of my left hand, and I pray that no one saw.

The snow is still wet and the air is cold and damp, the pavement sodden with clumps of melting ice. Above, the sky is a dismal grey, pressing down on me.

I walk quickly, trying to forget what is happening behind me in the cafe.

'Hey! Hey, you! Stop there!'

I pretend not to hear the voice over the thundering of the pulse in my head. I do not know who it is and do not want to know. It might be one of the Rights from inside, it might be a fellow Leftie, or it might be the cop.

'I said stop! Now!'

I do not here them. I repeat it to myself as I wade through the grey snow, head down, hands in my pockets.

I am not here, I tell myself. I am at home. I am in the other cafe with the girl. I am home watching television. I am with my parents. I am anywhere but here.

That is not the sound of metal sliding out from leather. That is not a click of greased mechanisms grinding across each other. A chamber being loaded.

That is not the strained, angry voice of an armed man who has already made his decision about me.

This not happening.

This is not the way things are.

It can't be.

THE DARK

I thought that I could see, but the path is dark.
I thought I knew the way, but I do not.
I found your hand and held it tight.
And I'll hold it, just as long as I can.
It helps me feel safe in the dark.
I have no torch, though for a long time I thought I did.
I thought I could see my way, but that seems now false.
Others say they can see, that they have their torch, have
earned their torch.
But now I suspect that their eyes are closed, and it is their
imagination that they see.
They imagine their way, and this is all they need.
I envy this.
But I know now; the path is not there.
It never was.
For all is dark.

Polythrenody

TOOTHBRUSH & PANTS

Can you keep a secret?

The cat asks a third time, despite me ignoring their previous attempts to elicit a reply from me.

The flywheel of my bicycle buzzes like a pursuant fly as I push it along the path of the park, handle-bars gripped on my left.

The cat trots along on the right, it's gait light and carefree, as though it doesn't care about the answer; taking pleasure simply in the asking of it.

I can feel the golden eyes staring up at me, and sense the inevitability of the inquiry being repeated a fourth time.

At this point, I'd like to make it clear that this is unusual for me. Cats, or any form of animal, domestic or otherwise, do not tend to start conversations with me.

The larger part of me is unwilling to encourage

whatever mental breakdown I appear to be having, but the idea of being asked again makes me uncomfortable. I mutter a reply self-consciously, 'No...'

The cats give a happy little meow and to my dismay cries, *Good!*

It then runs on ahead, darts across the lawn, hops up onto a wall and looks back at me. At that moment I have a sudden and disconcerting sense of familiarity. There is something in that look that rings a tiny bell in my mind.

Before it leaps out of sight, it gives me a sharp and knowing wink.

For the first time, I wonder if perhaps I should go home and get into my *own* bed.

I had entered the park, quite happily, having made better progress on my ride up the long hill, and had decided to walk the bike under the sunlit boughs. I was early, after all; barely seven-thirty, and did not want to seem too keen.

The situation with the cat had perturbed me, but I had decided to chalk it up to a week of stress at work. I'd started taking St Johns Wort and attempted to replace my seven cups of coffee a day with camomile tea, hoping that this weekend away from the escalating office tensions would relax me by Monday.

I needed to simply get out of my head.

Taylor's little flat was only a thirty-minute ride from my shared house, but far enough from the chaos of the city centre that to me, it was the Maldives.

I heave my bike up the steps and buzz the door. There is no voice over the intercom, but the lock clicks, allowing me to push my bike inside the vestibule where I lock it up.

I take the steps to the third floor two at a time and rap excitedly on the door. It crosses my mind that this might not be the right flat and check the address on my phone; no, it's correct.

Taylor and I had met three times before, having enjoyed the same number of successful dates that had resulted in an invitation to spend the weekend at her place. We had yet to sleep together, and although there had been implication to that effect in text form that had aroused in me an adolescent hope, it was not a given.

Taylor, despite being lovely and interesting, seemed bizarrely mercurial. In truth, I found her erratic personality deeply intriguing and was looking forward to the weekend.

She opens the door sharply, creating an odd backdraft that almost seems to want to pull me inside the flat. I prepare myself to say hi, but she has already leaned in to plant a kiss on my lips.

I respond, surprised, yet obviously pleased. Taylor had kissed me only once before, without me first initiating it; the other times she seemed either very reserved or extremely enthusiastic.

This time, it was gentle.

I jump. There is a quiet meowing and pressure against my shin. Opening one eye, I peer past Taylor's cheek to the floor and see a cat there.

My heart settles. It is not the same cat from the park; this one is dusty black, the one in the park was ginger. I admonish myself for the foolishness. It was a mild psychotic episode, that's all.

I hope that there was such a thing.

Taylor must sense my shifted attention, and breaks the kiss. She looks at the cat, frowns, shoes it away with her foot, then smiles, 'Are you coming in then?'

I cannot help but grin, 'Yes, please.'

Her eyes are blue; I hadn't noticed that before.

Taylor takes my hand and leads me inside. The black cat stalks away, glaring at Taylor. As she closes the door, I scan the corridor and see that on a little cushioned Ottoman there is another cat. This one is white and seems to be completely comatose, curled up and purring softly.

I shudder at the sight of yet another cat. Having never given the feline species much thought, I suddenly felt very wary around them.

Taylor's hand pulls me away, into the living room and thoughts of cats dissolve like sugar in water.

The black cat leaps on top of the Ottoman, beside the white cat that does not even flinch at the presence.

It would not. Could not.

With judgemental green eyes, she watches the two humans move into the living room, Taylor looking over the visitor's shoulder and giving a wink.

The black cat sighs and frowns in such a way that to any other species it might appear like an unchanged expression, then hears a rattle of pots in the kitchen.

Leaping off the Ottoman and trotting into the kitchen, they arrive in time to see the ginger Tabby shaking their paws convulsively at the dampness of the draining board.

They were, and always had been, the clumsiest. The tabby sees the black cat staring, *What?*

Polythrenody

Where have you been?

The tabby doesn't shrug in the conventional sense, but the implication is received, much to the black cat's irritation.

Sensing an incoming interrogation, the tabby changes the subject, *They're here?*

A nod that is not a nod.

The tabby drops from the worktop to the linoleum floor, sits and states matter of factly, *I want to go next.*

It's not your turn until tomorrow morning.

I want to swap.

The black cat sighs and turns her back, *We all agreed on the schedule. The buyer for the new model will be here soon, so I need to take control of the asset when they arrive.*

Oh yeah, the tabby retorts, ruefulness in their voice, *was that part of the agreement?*

The black cat follows the tabby's gaze to the gap in the living room door, to where the humans are busily removing their clothes.

Oh, for goodness sake.

It wasn't that it wasn't enjoyable, just unexpectedly brief, and Taylor had almost immediately fallen asleep.

And it wasn't the fact that she had pinned the left arm, it was nice that she felt comfortable enough to nod off, but that she suddenly felt like a dead weight.

The event over, any afterglow of satisfaction is smothered by the feeling of vulnerability in my semi-clothed state. I am at least pleased that although I had packed lightly, the left pocket of my jacket holstering my toothbrush and in the right, a spare pair of pants, I am smugly prepared for any and all eventualities.

I look around the flat. It is a hodgepodge of accumulated items and furniture rather than a space designed ahead of creation.

And there is an awful lot of cat hair, I notice for the first time.

It covers the carpet and most of the surfaces and even my recently discarded garments now have a fine layer of fur.

I detect movement in my peripheral vision and turn my head as far as I can in my awkward position. The white cat is waking up from its place on the Ottoman, yawning and stretching and giving me an odd, sort of pleased look before jumping to the floor.

It stalks away into the kitchen, to where the black cat is stood seemingly waiting for it with an air of contemptuous foot-tapping. The white cat rubs itself against the black, the latter seeming to become infuriated at the action and swiping its paw.

A third cat then appears, jumping between them and bats the door.

To my horror, I realise that it is the ginger cat from the park.

A feeling of unease washes over me as the door slowly closes, and it appears to me that the three cats begin to mew aggressively at one another like they're arguing over something.

I look at Taylor. She looks barely alive, her breathing so slow and shallow it's barely there, and I stroke her cheek. I expect a twitch or a murmur, or her blue eyes snapping open and smiling at me.

She doesn't even flinch.

I try it again.

Nothing.

It's like there is no one there.

There is a mewing noise and a shape appears beside me; the ginger cat is staring at me, having slipped away from the kitchen, and for a heart-stopping moment, I think it's going to speak.

It doesn't.

Instead, it walks around the back of the sofa, settles on the arm by Taylor's insert form and closes its eyes.

Polythrenody

There is silence, except for the sporadic, frantic meowing and clattering coming from the kitchen and the two brawling cats.

A sharp intake of breath.

Taylor's head suddenly lifts.

Her eyes still shut tight, she leans forward, lifts her arms and stretches like she's been asleep for longer than a few minutes, makes a satisfying sound that is almost a purr.

'Taylor?', I venture.

Her eyes open to look at me. They are light brown, almost golden. Were they always that colour? I find myself asking.

She moves sudden, turning towards me in a sharp jerk, alive with excitement and energy; different from the calm, gentle person who let me in moments before, or the cool, poised and intelligent woman with whom I had shared a glass of wine with the previous week.

Taylor studies my face, like she is reading my thoughts, then winks, and asks with wry amusement, 'Can you keep a secret?'

Polythrenody

THE SANDWICH

I am not a sandwich enthusiast, not by any stretch of the imagination. In most cases, I will be just as delighted by the simple pleasures of smooth strawberry jam on a supermarket own-brand white bread, as I am with an artisan four-cheese, caramelised onion and red pepper open-toasted on seeded rye.

Most days I can barely be bothered to throw together a mild cheese sandwich, let alone take the time and effort to add the pickle and lettuce required to create a ploughman's.

There are times that I just want a quick and easy snack, others where I just needed a functional yet satisfying meal on the run, and there are there those rare days that I just want to feel good about what I am consuming. I often eat alone, and yet relish in those rare moments in my busy life where I can enjoy a sandwich with friends, in either a casual manner or as part of a long-awaited event. A birthday for instance, or a wedding.

On those occasions, I like to really make an effort. I get a sense of purpose from it, from creating something really special, to appreciate myself, sure, but also to share. I like to have others comment on and compliment my sandwich. Not everyone will like it, and those people can be rather cruel, but I can live with it.

My sandwiches are for me, and me alone to enjoy.

This is the story of one of the days that I made a particularly amazing sandwich.

My friends and I had arranged to meet for drinks, and as the unspoken agreement, were each busy making out own sandwiches. We had in advance conversed and discussed our ideas for what gastronomic delight we might dream up and construct.

Devon was opting for something centred around salmon, which although raised eyebrows amongst our group, we all knew he'd probably do a good job of it and surprise us.

Heather had been quite cagey about her design but had hinted that she might do something with barbecue pulled-pork.

Awkwardly, both Santiago and Jerry had said very

little, but I had a suspicion that based on the individual chats I had, they might making the same ones.

I did not expect my creation, however, to be easily copied on account that I blending two entirely different yet popular sandwiches into one.

As I stood in my kitchen, golden late afternoon light streaming through the west-facing window, sliced into strips by the smoke from the grill-pan, I brought my creation to life.

Two slices of fresh sourdough bread were sliced and lightly toasted placed side by side and generously buttered.

A plump, blood-red beef tomato is severed into two; one half again severed, the remaining half stowed in my fridge. Likely to go off before I remember its there, causing a sudden recollection of its existence followed by disappointment at its new furry coat.

Lettuce leaves washed in cool water, placed on what will become the bottom slice, the tomato on its topside partner.

I smear luxurious and creamy coleslaw across the tomatoes and then add the first of the sandwiches focal points. Delicate strips of pastrami, streaky, red, flecked with cracked pepper, and atop them circles of spicy salami.

It is here that I become bold and smear just a little tomato relish. Some might argue that the combine this with the coleslaw is absurd, insane even, but I am and have always been, a culinary renegade.

It's addition to the project is not thoughtless whimsy, I hasten to add now, was a deeply considered part of the intricate construction.

From the still smoking pan, I carefully, as though carrying high explosive, a juicy slice of seasoned chicken thigh. Four strips in all, placed with the reverence one might grant the ark of the covenant, atop the already glistening bed of lettuce.

Then carefully, I take the loaded top half, ease it over, invert and settle it on the lower counterpart.

I press gently with my fingers, encouraging the layers to bond whilst ensuring that my digits to not shred the fragile bread.

To finish, I take my sharpest knife and let the edge do its work, dropping easily through so that I can now fully appreciate the splendour of the sandwiches several luscious strata.

The work done, I admire it for only a few moments before wrapping it in brown paper, so that only either end can be seen.

I know that I have spent an awfully long time here,

but I really just wanted to put across not only the majesty of what I have created, or the pride I felt as having breathed it into existence, but the simple that fact that I made just effort for myself.

Thoroughly pleased with myself, I head off at a trot across town to meet my friends.

The weather is warm and the sun is still some way from setting. In a few weeks, its heat will fade and the night will encroach sooner, but until then I planned to enjoy as many of these balmy days as I can.

My sandwich cradled in my hand, I catch from the corner of my eye the occasional look of approval or a sharp inhalation as its scent wafts behind me. I don't mind, I made the effort, and it's nice to feel that it has been noted.

I am good at making sandwiches, so I'd be lying if I said that I didn't mind compliments, even the more lewd grunts of, 'Nice sandwich, mate.'

Occasionally someone will ask for a bite, I just smile and ignore it and that is usually that.

Tonight, however, is not one of those nights.

The markets are a quieter part of town, situated between the bulk of the retail district and the canal where the nicest pub and open areas are. The high streets sort of circle the town like a brightly lit, busy girdle, but it adds an extra ten minutes to the walk. Nipping between the skeletal stalls, now closed for the day, their stock removed and packed away in warehouses somewhere, the market has a graveyard quality to it at this time of the day.

During working hours, the market is filled with bodies and noise and life, but now something is imposing about it.

Often, I pass through without a care and yet, today, cradling my sandwich, I feel oddly vulnerable.

I hear the voice at first, from ahead of me, creeping out of the mouth of a man sitting on the rail of what tomorrow will be a stall that sells babies clothes and schoolwear. Now, it looks like the carcass of a long-dead beast, the man who perches on the metal ribs cage, a vengeful wraith.

'That's a tasty looking sandwich,' he caws, his eyes dark and penetrating. They don't look at me, at my face, but at the prize in my hands.

I don't look at him, avoid meeting his lustful gaze. It is hard to know whether he truly like the look of my sandwich, or simply enjoys the sudden fear he has instilled in it. Perhaps one would add to the flavour of the other.

I hurry past and hear him inhale as the scent of the

sandwich hits him.

He growls, deep and throaty, a salacious sound emanating from deep with him.

'That smells lovely.'

I am past him. I don't need to respond, or react in any way because in moments I will at the crossing, then I will be over the main road and back into busy streets filled with wine bars and people.

But I hear him move. His heavy boots drop onto the flagstones and start a drumbeat of momentum behind me.

And he speaks again, his tone still playful, 'Gis' a bite, will you?'

I ignore him.

'Just one little nibble. Off the edge. I won't take a big bite. I only want to a little bit.'

He is only a step or so behind me, and he seems to radiate threat like heat. His proximity makes me feel like I need to reply, lest I seem rude and antagonise him.

'No thank you.'

I know it makes no sense, but the intention is there.

Then I see his form out f the corner of my eye, drawing alongside me. The road is a few steps further. There are no cars. A moment ago, in my head, it represented some sort of boundary that he would not be willing to cross. Now I understand that it is nothing of the sort.

He too seems to know this as he says, 'Don't be like that. I'm just being nice. I'm just saying that sandwich looks amazing, and I only want a little bite of it.'

My heart is beating fast now. My legs feel like jelly. The hand that holds my precious sandwich is becoming sweaty.

I say again, fear making my voice quiver, so I try to increase my volume, 'I said no thank you.'

It is then that things get out of hand, so to speak.

His tone changes, no longer playful, but annoyed, resentful and threatening, 'Why you being so fucking rude to me? Come on, just stop and give me a little a bite of it, then you can go. Eh? Just stay and let me have a bite or two. Go on.'

And then he reaches for it. I sense his claws, more than see them or feel them, sliding under my arm, touching the delicate fillings between the bread.

I jerk away instinctually, which only serves to further enrage him.

He grins at me through rotting teeth, although he is clearly becoming angry, and playfully lunges for my sandwich again. I yank it away, trying to dart towards the road, but he grabs my arm this time.

He is much stronger and spins me to face him, his large hand leaping into my arms, fingers like a tentacle, seeking out my sandwich.

I pull away, cry out, leap back but his talons have found purchase. I hear the brown paper tear, sensing the structure of the bread fail and the contents start to drift from one another.

Looking down, I see his dirty fingernails digging into the soft flesh of the sourdough, tearing it apart as I try to pull it in the opposite direction.

Inevitably, it falls to pieces. Chicken and tomato and pastrami and lettuce squashed together and ripped into chunks scatter and fall to the ground until I am left with a tattered husk in my palms.

On the other side of the road, I see, a few people are passing by, a group on the way to the park themselves, clutching their own sandwiches. They look over with interest, perhaps concern, but otherwise say nothing.

Their presence alone is enough for the man to slink away, back to the shadows of the market stalls. As he does, he grins at me and licks the sticky juice and flakes of debris from his fingers with crusty lips and a fat, obscene tongue.

Shaking, I hurry across the road, what remains of the

sandwich dropping in wet chunks from my hands. The group of people who are passing I can hear asking if I am okay, but I only mutter a reply and vanish from their sight.

At the park by the canal, my friends at once see my demeanour and my ruin sandwich still sticking to my hands and fingers. They a storm of concern for me and anger at my attacker as they hug me and clean me up.

They provide a drink and with shaking hands I sip it, retelling the story that seems suddenly so long ago, although taking place only minutes before.

Gradually, I am able to regain myself, to stop my hands and voice from shaking. The man's face and his voice, however, seem forever etched into my mind.

With bravery I do not truly feel, I declare I will not let it ruin the evening. My friends do their best to converse around the subject, but there is a cloud over the group now that is not helped by one, friend, whom I will not name because I know that no harm was meant by the comment, saying.

'You should have gone around. You should not have gone through the market. You should have known it was going to happen.'

In the end, I make my excuses and go home early. Santiago offers to go home with me, but I decline and take a taxi, rather than walk. It is a shame, the route is always a pleasant one that I enjoy regardless of the time of day. Right now, the thought of it fills me with dread, with or without a sandwich in my hand.

The following day Heather calls to check up on me, and I admit to her that the event had truly shaken me up. She offers to come round later and asks if I had yet called the police.

I know that sandwich theft is taken very seriously, and although my attacker did not manage to eat my sandwich, the fact that it was destroyed had taken its toll on me.

Still, I play it down, tell her that I'm alright and just want to forget about it.

For the rest of the day, I only eat toast and margarine. The idea of anything more turns my stomach.

I call my parents the day after to tell them, and to hear their voices. They are devastated and they insist that go round spend the night. We have lunch and go for a walk and for the most part, avoid the subject. It is in the evening when the wine is opened, that my dad's quiet fury spills out and there is talk of hunting the man down and gutting him. My mother is calmer, but I can see the anger boiling away inside, but later it becomes clear that the fury is not directed entirely at my attacker, but also with me.

'Why in gods name,' she asks me, tears prickling her eyes, her throat tight with emotion, 'Would you even think of going out with a sandwich like that? You know what people are like! They take one look at it and decide that it's there just for them! Promise that in the future, you'll be more sensible.'

Although I make the promise to end the conversation, I do not enjoy the company of my parents for the remainder of the evening and leave for home straight after breakfast.

The following week I keep myself as busy as I can, with work and chores at home and my friends, whom I encourage to visit me.

On those occasions that I do go out, I make only a very boring sandwich and keep it hidden well. After work on Wednesday, I meet Jerry for a quick drink after work, as is our routine. I put together a very tasty ploughmans' with smoked cheddar and shredded mozzarella with chilli jam rather than pickle. It is nice to make it and eat it with Jerry, but I was constantly on edge and was glad to have finished it.

It is a shame, I reflect later that night in bed, because the eating is the part I enjoy the most.

I do not sleep well, rerunning the incident through my

head, questioning my decisions, what I did or didn't do. Perhaps that is why I decide to finally go to the police, at least that is what I tell them.

Now, I know I shouldn't. But I know it was because I felt embarrassed.

Ashamed.

I call and they invite me in. The woman who takes my details is very nice and makes me feel at ease, but the pair of police officers who come to talk to me after are as cold and sterile as the room in which we sit.

One is a short, moustached man with a balding pate, the other a tall woman with broad shoulders and a pointed chin.

The questions are clinical, and they inform me there are numerous ongoing cases of sandwich assault and theft. I had thought that my memory of the incident was crystal clear, and the more they press me with questions as they try to "build up an image of the scene", I feel like I'm trying to fill in gaps in my recollection with guesses.

I can see them making assumptions of me now, seeming to take me less seriously the more they hear. They ask why I took so long to report it, and are obviously so dissatisfied with my answer that I simply felt embarrassed.

I leave the police station and catch the bus home, feeling so small that a bump in the road might send me flying from my seat and into the crack between the upholstery.

I am hungry, but cannot stand the thought of a sandwich, which saddens me. My passion is now something that instils anxiety in me.

No, I think to myself, watching the streets dash past me, filled with people who stride by, some holding sandwiches boldly or eating them right where they stand.

I will not be beaten by this. If I want a nice sandwich on occasion, I will damned well make one, and it'll be even better.

I just need to be smarter about it. My friend was right, my mother was right, and the police and their scepticism were right.

As the bus trundles me home, I start writing a list of rules in my head.

I will be careful where I take my sandwich.

I will only take my sandwich out during the daytime.

If I am going out with my sandwich, I will tell a friend where I am, where I am going and when I due to arrive.

Thumbing through my phone, I look for clues on

what other people have done to protect their beautiful sandwiches. Worryingly, a good proportion of the comments I find seem to believe that if you create a sandwich as amazing mine was, and you're simply asking for trouble. That people who make these sorts of sandwiches need to take responsibility for the repercussions on themselves.

I frown. This troubles me. It feels unfair.

I rest my head on the vibrating glass, let the buses relentless rhythm soothe me and I accept that which cannot, or will not, be changed.

It's just the way the world is, I guess.

Polythrenody

COW

I can see that she is trying really hard, but it is clear that I do not have her full attention.

Chewing my food slowly, I listen intently, making a concerted effort to maintain eye contact. It's my hope that if I do this, to show that I'm concentrating on what she is saying, it'll put her at ease.

It's not easy, that said. Listening to her is akin to twisting the dial on an analogue radio, the frequency shifting back and forth so that any information is disjointed and almost nonsensical. The fact that I'm staring at her so hard, I suddenly realised is having the opposite effect.

It's clear that she's lost her train of thought and the intensity of my gaze has put her off her stride completely.

She trails off, painfully embarrassed, and gives full

attention to slicing her barbecue hunter's chicken into strips. When she pops the chunks into her mouth and chews, her eyes once again flit up, past me, over my shoulder, at the cow stood silently behind me.

For the most part, I have learned to ignore it. In most aspects of my life, it's surprisingly easy to go about my business with very little impact.

It is, however, considerably more difficult to enjoy a romantic meal in a restaurant with a cow stood beside you.

It is a large, inelegant thing. Not the sweet black and white kind you see on the labels of milk cartons or the dusty-red shaggy type from the Scottish highlands.

My cow is a dirty grey, almost black. Its face seems to droop, pulling the skin down from around its dark eyes, around which there are always flies buzzing. Its tail is constantly swishing and its dirty hooves seem to be always shuffling, as if in a perpetual state of pins and needles.

I look at my dinner companion. She is quite lovely, quite petite, and almost mousy. Her name is Jayne and had met a few times queuing at the deli I frequent for my lunch. We had fallen into conversation after a customer ahead of us had gotten into a row with the owner regarding tomatoes. I forget exactly what the issue was but it had gotten quite heated, almost to the point of the police being called. Jayne and I had stood awkwardly together, watching the scene play out, and obviously took comfort in the fact that we weren't experiencing it alone. I'd noticed her on a handful of previous visits, but she hadn't become aware of me until that point. Thereafter, we always said hello until the day that I had purposefully timed my visit to clumsily ask her out for dinner.

In the deli, she had smiled and looked over at my cow. It was standing half in, half out of the shops' doorway, chewing noisily and staring at me.

At that point, I had decided that she was going to decline and that I was going to have to find a new deli, but she said that she'd like to.

Jayne works in a discount grocery store, so I had only seen her in casual workwear. She sits now in comfortable jeans and a stylish strappy top. Her brown hair, already very curly, seems to be more voluminous from whatever mysterious contraption women use, and her brown eyes seem different. Perhaps it's the mascara or fake lashes. I can't tell, but she looks nice.

And those eyes keep darting to my cow. It's clearly bothering her.

I sigh inwardly, sensing that this isn't going to go well.

There is a chattering noise, and the squirrel sat by her glass of wine nibbles come of the breadstick gifted to it earlier. On her lap is a large foppish rabbit that she absently mindedly strokes, and perched on the back of her chair is a large raven that stares contentiously at me.

The bird intimidates me, and yet I still find myself thinking jealously that I wish I had them, rather than my cow.

I have a stoat too, but I rarely see it, especially since the cow came along. The stoat has always been quite secretive, preferring to dart around in the shadows, even before. Once it used to cling to my shoulder, snarling at anyone who got too close, including the three butterflies and the dormouse that had been with me for almost as long I could remember.

I could no longer remember my first kiss, it was so long ago. I was 8 years old and it was barely a kiss, more a peck on my cheek from a classmate whom I do recall always made my stomach lurch when she sat by me during reading time. From then on, the first butterfly appeared and was my constant companion for the next few years until I reached my mid-teens.

It was Anna that I had always considered being my first real kiss. We were fifteen and awkward and both felt left behind by our respective friends. Mine at least seemed to have been drifting in and out of childish relationships since they were in year seven, and I had never honestly minded. In the preceding few months, however, just after my fifteenth birthday, I had started to wonder what it would be like to snog someone.

Anna was the same, and it was at a mutual friend's house party that, due to our virginal status, we were both embarrassingly encouraged to hook up.

Shoved into a tiny hallway at the bottom of the stairs, my dad waiting outside in the car to take me home, it was Anna who initiated it.

Her lips were cool and smooth on mine, and it was like no sensation I had ever felt before. I had no clue as to what I should be doing, and let her lead. Years later, I am aware of the painful awkwardness of the encounter, and the distinct lack of skill from both parties, yet it remained a fond memory. When we finished, my mouth tickled, something was fluttering against my tongue and when I opened it, a large red admiral butterfly flew out.

My third kiss was a drunken one when I was seventeen, in those wonderful years when it was far easier to get into nightclubs underage. I never knew her name, barely recall her face, but her skill was undeniable. For those few minutes, I transcended space and time, existing outside of my own body, my nose filled with her sweat and perfume, my mouth with her probing tongue.

I returned to earth with a bump to find her gone, my friends in hysterics and myself sporting a horrendously obvious erection.

Butterflies, even three of them, do not interfere with your life too much. They flutter about your head, sometimes flitting away in the sky, all but forgotten, then suddenly their delicate little wings are batting against your cheek, just for a moment.

My dormouse I miss the most. A sweet and innocent little thing that sat contentedly yet quietly on my shoulder, occasionally nuzzling my ear yet seemed to be happy simply watching me live my life.

The stoat that appeared years after, devoured them, one by one, until they were all but forgotten. In time, my stoat seemed to relax and be satisfied to sneer from dark corners. For a few years, I could almost pretend that it wasn't there.

Then the cow came, and there was no pretending anymore.

Jayne is nervous. The rabbit on her knee suddenly kicks out furiously and she has to tighten her grip to keep it from bounding of her knee and under the feet of the waiting staff.

I look around. I really want this to go well. It has been a long time since I have put myself out there like this. It's hard to date with a cow bumping you all the time.

We are in a gastro pub not far from her house, that I suggested so that she did not have to travel too far. She protested but seemed to appreciate the thought. It occurred to em after though, I hope she wasn't feeling awkward in case she bumped into people that she knew.

I have to rescue this somehow. We're already finishing our main course and I had presumptuously ordered dessert.

Shit, I should not have ordered dessert.

I panic, top up my glass of wine and offer her more. Jayne nods gratefully, and we both drink immediately, clearly trying to sip, not gulp.

Casting my mind back to our casual, easy conversations in the deli, for clues as to conversational topics. It was so easy then, with no expectations, no judgment, to projections or risks or insinuations or misunderstood questions.

I don't ask anything, instead offer my own information based on one of her comments, and tell her about my five-year-old son.

Immediately the cow bellows, its hollow screech echoing across the restaurant and my stomach lurches.

Fucking cow.

Then it shuffles, its great weight knocking my chair, making me spill my wine down my shirt. I was trying to hold it so coolly as if I drank wine all the time. I wasn't and didn't.

I am mortified as I use my paper napkin to dab down my shirt, thanking my good fortune that it was pinot grigio, not noir.

Looking back at her, I see her stifling a giggle. She has a lovely smile, her teeth flash then she presses them together in a sweet little pursing thing.

It makes me smile.

She smiles wider, then takes pity on me by not mentioning my accident. Instead, she tells me about her work as a retail assistant in a self-deprecating manner that is wonderfully endearing.

The rabbit kicks against. This time she does not restrain it and lets it jump from her lap and under the table. I can feel it trampling over my shoes there, but it doesn't bother me.

Jayne is smiling and telling me about her son's interests in fossils, and I tell her my own has an obsession for insects.

Our topics meander back and forth, sprawling across dessert and three new round of drinks. Not wine, I am pleased to say. Eventually, we find ourselves on the only conversational path where all other routes inevitably lead to.

Five years, she tells me, and then she is brutally candid. Never married, but the baby that she and her partner conceived together died in the second trimester. Their relationship did not survive the ordeal, grief driving a wedge between them.

The rabbit is suddenly back on her lap, leaping clumsily into place, strong back legs kicking out furiously, dragging the table cloth, sloshing my pint of Fosters.

I take a deep breath. The cow is moving, its big, stupid head banging into mine, leaning over the table, and sticking its fat, disgusting tongue into my pint. It doesn't even like Fosters.

I put my hand on its face, try to push it away, as I submit my own report.

Fifteen years, twelve married. She wanted more kids, I wanted to travel.

Jayne finds my cow's alcoholism amusing, yet she seems troubled.

She asks if I was done having children. I feel this is a make-or-break moment. I like her, but I need to stay true to myself. I don't want to scare her away so soon that I am prevented from the opportunity to learn more of her, or her of me.

I sidestepped, but answer with honesty. Not with her.

Holding my breath as she considers my reply, my cow now deciding is the time that my hair needs to be licked clean.

Jayne smiles and says that she has had a lovely night, but she needs to go home and relieve the babysitter.

We stand together, animals scurrying around our feet or flying overhead, my cow lurching after us and my stoat somewhere in the shadows, as we make our way through the restaurant to the entrance.

We spend a few minutes enjoying each other's company in the cold night air, me drinking in her smile until she says that she really should go, and does.

There is no kiss. I fear it is because my cow saw fit to lick my face just moments before.

We walk home in silence, my cow and I. Sometimes I talk to it. I recount the date, tell it where I think I smashed it and where I went wrong, what was wrong with her, or me, or why it wouldn't work. It is the hired date I've been on since the cow appeared.

Each one of my prospective partners has sat and stared at the hairy, dirty bovine stood beside me, and not one of them has granted me a second date.

I do not talk tonight. My cow seems to miss the chat, and nudges my arm. My throat tightens up, my fists clench. I am angry.

I tell the cow, in no uncertain term, to fuck off.

This is new. I have never done this before. I have simply accepted its presence and gotten on with my life, as best as you can when a half-ton beast is on your heels.

The cow huffs but continues to butt my arm with his head, harder and harder, each impact raising the temperature of my blood.

I run.

My shoes are slippery and loud, not suited to any form of exercise, and yet I do not stop until I have reached my flat.

I fly up the stairs, barrel through my door, lock it and get into bed. There I lie, sleep refusing to stop by and do its thing, so scroll through the day's events on social media.

With dreadful inevitability, I hear the front door being battered. The wood sheers, the glass smashes and then the click-clacking of filthy hooves on my tiled kitchen floor.

A moment later, the bedroom door is pushed open and the cow stands there, staring blankly in at me.

I turn over, close my eyes and try, unsuccessfully to ignore it.

Jayne and I do not go out for dinner again. I don't know if she keeps going to the deli, because I find a new place further up the high street. She does not call or text me, nor I, her.

I wonder if my cow is the issue, and not the presence cow itself, unwanted though it is, and not even Jaynes less than favourable reaction to it.

It's the contrast, I find myself thinking over the next few days. It's the difference between mine, and hers.

Jayne's animals are so *small*. Sure, she is younger, so it makes sense, but the three of those little creatures would sit on the back of my cow and it wouldn't even know that they are there.

With guilt, I come to realise that this is an issue for *me*. I tell myself it doesn't matter, and almost believe it. To a degree, it does not, because my sister sets me up with one of her colleagues from her solicitors' office.

Her name is Pattie and she too stares at my cow, with one key difference; she seems to love my cow.

We had met for casual drinks, rather than a meal, and Patties eyes lit up the moment she lay eyes on it. She walked right up and stroked it, spoke to it, even hugged it, and only then did she turn and hug me tightly.

I'll spare the details, because the truth is, they are quite mundane. Pattie was quite wonderful from the start. Vivacious, with a lively mind, a sharp tongue, a loud, infectious laugh, and a penchant to hug for almost any reason.

Pattie has a bear. A huge thing, with great folds of shaggy red-brown fur that is so glossy it appears to give off its own light. It has great paws and an enormous head with little brown eyes that look at you with all the threat of a golden retriever puppy. That's not to say that it wouldn't be dangerous if provoked, it has yawned often enough to display a gaping maw that I could easily fit my head inside.

Other animals follow Pattie, but I have barely seen them. They are mice, or voles, or something like that. There is a handful of them, and bury themselves inside the bear's coat of fur and scurry about its body residents in a block of flats. They seem to feed off its warmth and take food from its mouth, having forgotten how to survive without it.

It takes only a few months for Pattie and I to go from a drink a few times a week, to her having a drawer in my bedroom, to my moving in with her.

Our relationship is one of great comfort and ease. We share bottles of wine on the sofa, watch Netflix series together and cook greats feasts on those occasions that our families are under the same roof. Her three daughters take to my young son like he was a new toy, and he loved being doted on.

My time becomes our time, and she is this great blanket of comfort across my shoulders, where for much of my adult life, I felt cold. I snuggle into the boundless and seemingly infinite love she showers me with. I enjoy my job more, tedious though it is, and look forward to coming home to her. We talk of our days, we relax with wine and television, we have long sessions of comfortable, satisfying sex and I sleep deeply.

I have never known an animal like her bear, so unlike any animal that I have encountered before. When we cook, it sits and gazes at us, bellowing softly as we talk, as though joining in. When we sit in front of the television, it drags its great plush bulk onto the sofa and lays with us, like a shaggy beanbag. There have been times where we have even used it as such. It never seems to mind. The bear seems to thrive on being a part of our relationship.

Throughout it all, my cow, dirty, cold, impassive, and clumsy as ever, stands and stares dully at me. It is then that I notice the rancid stink of my bovine companion and the almost sweet scent of the bear that fills any room it enters.

Inevitably, Pattie and I fall into talking of our ex-partners, surprisingly late in our relationship. We had of course informed one another of them, alluded to them, referenced them in passing, but I had only the faintest notion of my predecessor.

It turns out that Pattie had numerous small relationships throughout her twenties, each lasting a matter of months, as well as a string of sexual encounters that, she said, she enjoyed, felt that she was always missing something. Geoff had changed that, she said. Their relationship had grown slowly, spanning ten years before they married and had their first daughter. Pattie said it was because they had known each other, as friends of a mutual acquaintance, since they were children themselves. Her best friend's step-sister was his cousin.

Pattie said that it was a relationship that filled in all the gaps that she did not know were there. Her emotional needs were met, he was kind and generous and giving without any sense of debt, and would graciously and excitedly accept her gifts of affection in return. They grew a side business together, travelled extensively as a couple as well as a family of five when their twin daughters came along.

They had, what many had termed, the perfect relationship and even when they separated and took up with new partners, their friendship not only persisted but grew stronger. Now, as an expanded family, Pattie, Geoff, their three daughters, and her then-boyfriend, his husband and stepson, existed as a wonderful, fluid family commune, living minutes from one another.

Geoff had died three years before my meeting Pattie, tragically succumbing to injuries sustained paragliding in the alps. Pattie told me that he regretted nothing of his life, thanked his stars for meeting her and having children with her, and passed on surrounded by those he loved.

It was hard to ignore the radiant glory of this chapter in Pattie's life as she told it, her bear laying across us, heavy, hot, and breathing softly as it slept.

Polythrenody

I have my son every other weekend, and 2 alternating days during the off weeks. This allows time for me and my ex to have time with our son, and also enjoy our free time. We had long talked of the freedom of having a child within broken marriage, sharing custody meant that we weren't committed twenty-four-seven to the traditional family paradigm. We said how sad this was that we felt this way, and also how sad it was that others felt obligated to stick to the societal model.

I had concluded that it didn't matter, that the path that each person took was unique, and was walked in their own manner.

I sit in my ex's kitchen. Louise chases around after my son, getting him to tidy away his toys and pack what he needs for his weekend with me.

A cup of tea, going cold between my hands, I sit and watch the sea lion in the corner. It might be considered to be an odd place for a sea lion to be, but I'm used to seeing it when I see Louise. It appeared to Louise when my cow appeared for me, and like my cow, it lumbers after her, knocking over chairs, bumping into people, and generally getting in the way. Other than that, it does very little, despite its almost constant displays of noise and directionless enthusiasm.

Surprisingly, it has very little interest in me and usually

seems to barely register my existence unless I have food in my hands.

Right now, I have only tea. The sea lion does not like tea.

It stares at Louise, mouth agape, barking excitedly at Louise as she walks by, busily corralling our son. All it seems to want is her attention, and she refuses to provide it.

There is a knock at the front door, and I look to Louise to see if she wants me to answer it. Immediately there is a female voice from the corridor, and Ellen scuttles in. Her eyes widen briefly as she regards me, surprised, then smiles and greets me with tepid warmth.

She is Louise's best friend, and they have a weekend of drinking, pampering, and more drinking in mind. Ellen has an overnight bag that she drops onto the kitchen table across from me.

As we exchange pleasantries, I hear the lethargic clacking of paws on the tiled floor. A little head, long and brown peek around the corner, brown forlorn eyes make the briefest of eye contact with me, then the head withdraws.

I have only glimpsed the wretched excuse for a dog that follows Ellen around. I know only that it is a muddy brown with grey, perhaps once white, patches.

Its dull fur is clumpy and unbrushed, its waist so thin that its ribs are almost a percussion instrument and there always seems to be some sore or wound somewhere on its scrawny body.

The neurotic pooch will go nowhere near anybody, hiding under tables or chairs, staring at Ellen as though begging her to return to it, to keep it safe. Whenever she does, or anyone for that matter, it growls and yelps as though it is being beaten.

Ellen has been single for quite some time.

She and I had gotten on well throughout Louise and mines marriage, and I had briefly considered dating her, but the fact that it was Louise's friend made it a poor option for the sake of our already strained family dynamic.

I make conversation with Ellen. Her dog cowers in the corner, my cow gets in the way and stares at me as it chews loudly, but it is Louise's noisy, lazy sea lion that bothers me more than it usually does.

For some reason, as Ellen talks at me about something that had happened to her that day, I find myself thinking of Pattie's bear.

A bear whose presence I once found warm and inviting, I now find overwhelming and claustrophobic and intimidating. It looks down on me, I realise, and behind those colossal layers of glossy fur, there is a smile that says only one thing.

You will never be good enough.

I spend a nice weekend with my son. We have pizza out and go to the zoo, watch the monsters movies that he seems to enjoy and when I drop him back at Louise's on Monday, I come to a realisation that I have barely been present.

Guilt overwhelms me, and I hope that he has not noticed. I promise that the next weekend that I have him, I will be better.

I also know exactly the reason for my mental and emotionless displacement.

The following morning, a year, almost to the day, I break up with Pattie.

I expected anger. What I got was fury. She screamed and cried and threw things, and as she did her bear rose onto its hind legs and that great jaw opened wide to release a bellow that echoed through my whole body.

I spent an hour with her, in agony at seeing her in pain, wanting to throw my arms around her and make her feel better. That had, after all, been my job for twelve months and yet, even when she pleaded with me to just rethink, I found that I could not.

Pattie said that what stung her the most was the suddenness of it.

It was then that I went very quiet. For me, it was not sudden, I had come to realise the day before.

In the past few months, I had been returning to the deli where I met Jayne. I had no purpose, no grand plan and certainly no intentions of starting an illicit affair with her.

I simply had this compulsion to see her again.

Jayne had not appeared. It was clear that she too had deigned to chose an alternative vendor for her lunches, so I had stopped.

Yet, there was now something hanging over my relationship with Pattie that I could not articulate. Not then, and certainly not when asked that question by Pattie herself.

As a result, I left under a hail of broken crockery with the person whom I had professed to love for a year crying out for a closure she would never get.

I am on the tram going home, my ears still ringing with the hurtful things that my now ex-girlfriend had bombarded me with. It rattles and hums along the tracks, and there is the gentle purring of a cat on the seat opposite me besides a man in his fifties. On his shoulder, a racoon that yawns repeatedly.

A couple gets on and swears under their breath as they push past the bulk of my cow, stood, as usual, in the way of everything. The sound of it's chewing in my ear sets my own teeth on edge.

That's when I feel it. Something else. Pushing and pressing against my heels, beneath the seat. It does not move like anything I'd felt before. It sort of falls this way and that, thudding against my calves in waves. It feels big.

It stops, and I hope that it belongs to someone else.

Then I sense it behind me, slipping up the gaps between the seat and the trams walls until it bumps into my neck and starts to slide across my shoulders.

It squirms and coils itself across me, a forked tongue flicking out from the small head, the body thick and oily and impossibly long.

The snake is about a metre and a half long and weighs more than I thought it would when I stand to get off the tram.

As I carry its bulk home with me, I think to myself, thank goodness I broke up with Pattie when I did.

Throughout the following few weeks, I deal with the more practical aspects of ending a serious relationship. Having moved into her place, I had rented my own flat to a couple who were now expecting their first child. As a result, felt disinclined to boot them out and reclaim my home. For the first time, I began to regret my impulsive decision to end things with Pattie. It would have been more practical to have sorted a few things out first, such as where I was going to live or put the many items of furniture that I had moved into Patties.

I hired a storage unit. Pattie made herself scarce when I booked a moving van and spent a morning with my friend removing wardrobes, tables, a desk, an Ottoman, several lamps, my television, computer and various boxes of knick-knacks and clothes.

The house that Pattie and I shared looked heartbreakingly empty when I had finished.

That same friend put me up for a few nights, but his boyfriend quickly grew tired of me and so I found a place on Louise's sofa. For a week, my son was happy to see me every morning, but Louise less so. We were swiftly reminded of why our marriage was never going to last, something we discussed like rational adults, with kind words laced an undertone of unresolved resentment.

I had the foresight however of applying immediately for a short-term room in a house share, which allowed me my own space. It was tight, of course, with myself, my new snake the lumbering cow in a room only twelve foot by twelve foot. Usually, it stood in the doorway to chew and stink and stare at me all night, but in the dynamic of a house with strangers, could only stand right by my bed.

I barely slept for nearly a month.

At that time, I fell into a funk. I spent as much time as I could at work, and yet it couldn't occupy all my time and the evenings felt long. The onset of winter and the days becoming shorter only added to the sense of endlessness, sat in my tiny room, watching Netflix with a fat snake coiled on my bed, an enormous cow stood leaning over me.

Naturally, there were times when I longed to go home, and by that, I mean to Patties. To climb into her bead and to be wrapped up in her arms, where it was warm and safe and I knew that I was loved.

I questioned endlessly why I had ended and still, I had no real answer, but when I thought of calling her, I found my hand would not pick up the phone.

I did, however, think of calling Jayne.

I thought about it a lot.

And still, I did not. Every time I got close, I felt that cow staring at me, and now the snake too coiled itself around my ankles.

That said, in time, the snake began clinging to me less. Whereas the cow followed me without fail wherever I went, causing disruption and chaos all around me, the snake seemed more and more content to stay behind on my bed and sleep.

The cow. The fucking cow was everywhere.

It was there when I went to work when I went for rare drinks with my friends. It was around when I tried to catch the eye of the girl at the bar, or when I managed to engage one in conversation. It was there I went to sleep, when I woke, ate, watched television or had a shit.

It lumbered after me and no matter how hard I tried to run head and lose it, it would always find me.

And it was there when I finally ran into Jayne again.

The high street was busy, as it always was on a Saturday morning. Even with the threat of online shopping looming like a dark cloud across the retail industry, the town was still packed with throngs of shoppers and their pursuant animals.

If you decide to run the gauntlet of the narrow pedestrianised street, you accept the fact that you're going to be jostled not only by people who always seemed to have a contradictory gait and trajectory to yourself but their animals too.

Racoons and cats and weasels scurry amidst a veritable carpet of rodents darting to keep up with their humans. Mid-sized animals, from the dogs and pumas, to the bears, the lions and the gazelle pad or trot by, seemingly more aware of their spacial awareness. It is the largest animals that cause the most issue, for which there are blessedly few. The only really large animal I see regularly follows an old man, well into his 80's, and sadly, recently a widower.

Shuffling along to match his pace is an enormous African elephant. For such a behemoth, it is surprisingly aware of its surroundings and steps gently between people and other creatures. It seems to keep a watchful eye on its human with dark, intelligent eyes. I have even seen it guide the old man when he seems lost, or drape a comforting trunk across his shoulder when he appears confused.

I am watching them now. The old man is about to cross the road. One hand in on his cane, the other is pressed gently against the leathery grey skin of the elephant.

The traffic lights turn red. The cars stop. The silhouette of a man lights up green. The old man and the elephant cross slowly together.

I watch with envious eyes as my cow bumps me again, it's great bulk knocking me two steps and I feel my stomach clench. For an animal so much smaller than the elephant, the cow is not only infuriatingly more clumsy but skittish. Other animals and sometimes people seem to surprise it as if shocked to become suddenly aware of the existences of a creature other than itself. It leaps, if such a galumphing movement can be described as such, to the side, those rolling, dumb eyes rolling around so much as to expose the whites.

A lion has stalked by, a companion to a tall and athletic man, growling beneath its breath it's glorious mane shaking.

The cow leaps sideways, loses it's footing on its hooves and almost sends me into a woman flanked by a cackling hyena and an elegant yet skittish doe. She shoots me a cold look and filled with sudden ire, I shove my cow.

My feeble strength is lost on its great weight, which

only serves to infuriate me more.

I catch my temper in time. Unwilling to show me up in public, I swallow my frustration like a lump of hot coal.

It squeezes it's way down my throat with searing agony and drops into my belly where it continues to sizzle in darkness.

Jayne calls my name then, and as I spin to face her, I pray that she did not bear witness to my pathetic tantrum.

I must have turned with something resembling aggression because she seems to baulk, nearly taking a step away. I try to smile, to soften the hardness of my expression. There is a chance, however, that it came off as creepy.

She is gorgeous. She has no make-up on and her face is pale, slightly blotchy, under her eyes are dark and her nose looks a little red. Her lips seem thinner than I'd seen them before, on our date or at the deli before that. Jayne wears matching jogging bottoms and hoodie, pale pink and grey, with oversized comfortable boots, and her hair is tied back in a tight ponytail.

She is clearly self-conscious at being dressed so far down. As soon as I look at her, she holds my gaze only for a second before looking away, pulling at her hoodie and smoothing her hair, perhaps wishing it wasn't pulled back so tautly.

But it is her. It is a face that I had longed to see again since our date over a year ago, and as I look at her the chaos of the high street melts away.

I ask her how she has been and barely listen to watch she says, just happy to hear the sound of her voice. I must have heard something because I reply based on some exchange of information, and she asks me how I have been and I give her a brief and cursory answer that doesn't impart much.

I am nervous, I realise, as we stand in the street and chat. Far more so than I was on our first date. Then I was just excited, to talk, to get to know her, to spend time with her. This time I am very aware that, based on the result of last time, I could lose her again very quickly.

Very easily.

My conversational charm must be waning because her eyes soon fall to the dark, bulky shape behind me.

Fuck, she's looking at the cow.

I am then aware of the rabbit pawing at her calf, wanting to be picked up. She ignores it, keeping telling me of her work, but her eyes are still locked on my cow.

Polythrenody

And the cow nudged me with it behind, trying to turn around in the street behind me.

There is a jaguar, skulking by and snarling at everything it passes. My cow bellows and tries to move away from it, bumping into people and other animals as it does. There is the wave of curses and tuts and I apologize, first to them, then to Jayne.

She smiles and says it is okay, but now my cow is trying to step away from a group of loud teenagers who walk by, knocking them first, then me, until it is between me and Jayne.

I grit my teeth, trying to keep that hot ball of anger deep down in my belly. Jayne steps back, trying to get stepped on, still smiling, but now she has picked her rabbit up, to stop it from being trampled.

I apologise for my cow again, make some sort of half-formed joke, try to pull it back, away from her. It is too heavy. I don't know why I tried. Instead, I grab it around the neck, try to pull it head away with the hope its body will follow, then slip beneath it, back to Jayne. The cow tenses and pulls away from me. I pull harder, grabs its face and those big stupid fucking eyes look at me in confusion and I want to punch its stupid face.

I don't. I yank at it, and it yanks away, so hard that its own weight makes it stumble sideways.

Polythrenody

The cow crashes into Jayne, knocks her away, into the crowds and to the ground.

I manage to get around the cow and offer to help her up, but she is already on her feet.

She says that she is fine, but I can see that she is winded.

Jayne says that it was nice to see me, and although she seems to mean it, she leaves quickly.

I stand and watch her fade into the crowds, her and her rabbit and the squirrel and the crow.

I have run home, to the shared house. I lock the door and sit on my bed, hot tears in my eyes, my chest is tight and aching. I clenched my fists and open them. I want to crush something in them. I want to destroy something. I want to hurt. I want to be hurt. I want to feel pain in a place other than my heart.

Am I in love with Jayne? I don't know, but I know that she is in my thoughts and I'd like the chance to find out. But that fucking cow is always there, getting in the way and fucking everything up.

I had moved so fast that I had easily outrun it, and although it is hours before it lumbers up the stairs, it still finds me.

I hear it walk into the door, and ignore it. The panels rattle as it nudges them, and I can picture it knocking its head again the door, trying to get it to open. Over and over, again and again, too stupid to even realise that it won't work.

I ignore it for twenty minutes or more until my housemates tire of the noise and start shouting through the walls, telling me to let it in.

Oh, I'll let it in, I think. I storm across the room, unlock the door and open it with such force that the cow it startled.

It almost falls inside, eyes wide and flitting about. It stumbles one way, then the other. It pins me painfully against the bed, then as it tries to right itself, falls against the window.

The blind is ripped from its screws, plaster and paint raining down on the cows back and onto my bed. The blind clatter across it, broken and tattered and I finally lose the final fragment of restraint I had been clinging onto.

I tear the blind from its back, ripping it in two and find my hand is raised.

It comes down hard, and fast, and mean.

As it impacts, the cow lets out a bemused low and shakes its big head. My hand strikes again, the broken blind something between a stick and whip that feels good in my hand.

This time I see that it leaves a mark on the cows dark back and it bellows at me and I feel all the rage and frustration and disappointment and resentment hit me all at once. I am hitting it, again and again, and I cannot stop. No matter how much it bellows at me, or how much it throws it bulk this way and that, knocking over the bedside table, shoving the bed aside, fracturing the plaster wall, I don't stop.

I have no control. I wished that cow never existed. I want it to stop existing.

I don't stop. My housemates have gathered, watching or shouting at me, pleading to cease, but my attack only concludes when the cow charges out of the room.

It almost falls down the stairs in its panic, leaving stripes of smeared blood on the walls as it does, and me with a broken blind dripping with red.

On the bed, the snake stirs and starts to writhe, as though stretching sleep from its coils. It flicks its tongue and stares coldly at me.

I try to tidy my room. I wipe the blood away, wash everything fabric and bin that which can't be saved. I shower and change and go downstairs to make my dinner.

In the shared kitchen, my housemates avoid me, either through fear or disgust at my actions. I don't care. I feel lighter. I can barely feel my own weight and the light that comes through the window is beautiful to me.

I decide I do not want to be here, not just to eat, but to live. I'm going to go to the local pub, one of the cheap 2 for 1 on certain parts of the menu types. I'm going have two meals and two desserts all to myself, and as I unapologetically gorge myself, I'm going to check the online classifieds for a flat of my own. If I move some money around, borrow a bit here and there, I can accumulate a sizeable deposit within weeks.

My own place, and no cow.

I reflect on how utterly divine this sounds as I strut down the street towards the pub. I imagine this perfect scenario where I wake up to the smell of fresh coffee bubbling in the peculator that I'm going to buy, not the rancid, back-of-the-throat farmyard stench of the cow. I walk to the kitchen without having to push my way past its concrete-like flanks. I sit and eat my breakfast; pancakes with bacon and maple syrup, without the foul bovine breathing and chewing in my ear. I go out, to work and interact with any other human being without fear of my lumbering, intrusive cow getting in the way, or drawing their attention away from what I actually want to say.

Or do.

And finally, I return home and start dinner, able to move freely around my own home. The chips have just gone in the fryer and the ribeye steaks, freshly tenderised, seasoned and marinaded are waiting by the smoking pan, ready for when Jayne walk in.

I frown to myself, intrigued by how Jayne had appeared in my fantasy. As I draw closer to the pub, I allow that idea to take seed and bloom, to spread and stretch its tendrils out to every corner of my little made-up world.

Entering the pub doors, the welcome sickly-sweet scent of food, alcohol and carpet freshener hitting me, I realised that I would very much like Jayne to be in my future.

Fuck that; my present.

Perhaps I am still giddy from the sudden lack of bovine presence in my life, but I take out my phone, hammer in a text with my thumbs and hit send.

Then and only then do I realise how recklessly impetuous I have just been.

Polythrenody

I read the text back again.

Hey, it was great seeing you earlier. I'm at Horn &
Hammer if you fancy a quack drink? X

I'm not sure if I'm more horrified by the glaring
spelling error or the addition of the kiss at the end.
And it's so abrupt, and out of the blue, and what if
she's says no, or worse, doesn't reply at all.

When asked what I want to drink my the barman, I
stutter my order and stand there dumb when he asks
for payment.

Sloshing my pint as I cross to a table, I sit and stare at
my message in the chat list. The little tick has turned
from passive blue to blue, indicating that it has been
received.

I am about to look at the menu, although my appetite
has suddenly vanished without a trace. If anything, I
feel more likely to return items from my stomach,
rather than add to it.

A second little blue tick appears.

She's seen it.

Nothing.

Aeons pass. Civilisations rise and falls, continents drift
across the oceans and whole species evolve and are
wiped out.

Just as I resign myself to the fact that she isn't going to

reply, with a low chime, her reply comes back in.

Sounds lovely. Can you give me 45 minutes though? x

My heart stops, takes the time to read the message itself before continuing to beat. I reply casually, but the truth is if she said next week, I wouldn't move from this seat until then.

In the end, it is a little over an hour before she arrives, and I spend the time doing nothing more than having a hundred variations of our imminent conversation. How I say *hi*, do I hug her, kiss her cheek, pull out her chair or play it cool and don't stand up, or do I buy her a drink ready, or get it when she arrives. I am far more nervous than on our first date. Is this even a date? Fuck, what if it's not?

I have finished my pint, and although I am now dying of thirst through anxiety, refuse to risk lowered inhibitions by having another before she gets here.

The door to the pub opens. I have had the same reactions thirty-six times already, heart-pounding, stupid grin, sitting up, but this time it is her.

The crow flutters in first, circling the low ceiling and settling on the chair opposite me, where it's dark, judging eyes settle on me. The squirrel and the rabbit scurry and lope in together. The latter immediately leaps onto the table and sits to join the panel of judgement, whilst the rabbit seems to get lost and confused.

Jayne scoops it up. It kicks out for a second, then settles into her arms. She looks around and sees me, smiles with a warm that I feel in my belly.

Her hair and make-up are done, but in jeans and a denim jacket over a white band t-shirt, she looks very casual but stunning.

I realised, quite suddenly and brutally, that I am anything but dressed up. The spontaneity of my invite might be seen as romantic, but it was also incredibly impractical. I also conclude that I had realised this, I could have raced home, changed and come back in plenty of time.

Shit. In jogging bottoms and an ill-fitting shirt, I must look like a right mess.

If Jayne feels this, she hides it well. If I didn't know any better, I'd say that she didn't mind at all.

Thankfully, it is she who speaks first, sitting quickly and keeping the rabbit on her lap. It seems like it does not want to be put down. Like it's guarding her. I remember this from our date over a year ago.

I look at Jayne. Her lovely eyes are moving around the pubs interior, as though looking for something.

I know what she's looking for.

Quickly, I ask how she's been, trying to avoid talking of the incident earlier that day. We fall into easy conversation, in which she says she noticed the spelling error and wanted to reply in kind, but couldn't think of anything to do with ducks. She drinks vodka and orange and I have another pint that I drink slowly, to allow her to catch up. We order from the menu, although not from the 2 for 1 section, and wait for our food to arrive without a break in dialogue. The more comfortable we get, the more I notice the rabbit getting fidgety. After a while, she puts the rabbit on the floor. It paws at her, but she ignores it, or placates it and finally settles by her feet.

The impromptu date is comfortable and easy and exciting and I am a bundle of sparking nerve endings, yet I notice one thing.

I still do not have all of Jaynes attention. Her eyes still wander, as much as they did on our first date. This time they are not looking *at* my cow, so much as *for* it. Finally, she does ask where it is.

My reply seems almost defensive, stating proudly that I got rid of it.

This seems to confuse her, and she repeats it back to me.

Hearing it, it sounds absurd.

I got rid of it.

Jayne questions how that is even possible. She seems perturbed, unsettled by it, deeply concerned. Her eyes are soft, but they accuse and I feel suddenly very guilty. Perhaps it is the third pint or her gentle quality that makes me want to tell her anything. I blurt it all out.

My anxiety on the first date, her staring at my huge, lumbering beast and being put off by it. The fact that it overwhelms everything I do, is everywhere, affects everything and everyone around me and no matter what I do, it is there. It overshadows, infiltrates and at times, destroys. I do not mean to, but I tell her about the incident earlier, what I did to the poor creature and its escape from me.

When I am done she is frowning. I am terrified that she is furious at me.

After a moment, she reaches out and puts her hand on me and tells me that although there is no excuse for doing what I have done to the cow, she understands.

Then she allows a small smile, then says slowly that she was not scared of the cow on our first date, but she was intimidated by it.

It is so big, clumsy and dumb, for sure, but in its great size, there is something solid and majestic, built on years of friendship and experience. In those dull eyes there is history, and in those muscular flanks, strength. For someone who's animals are so small, so skittish or insecure in their diminutive size, it's hard to be faced with something like that.

But that, Jayne says, is *her* issue. She picks up her rabbit again, strokes it and for the first time, I see the affection that she has for it and all her animals.

They are a part of her, whether she likes it or not. She has not only accepted that they are but has welcomed them. Beyond this, she knows that she will certainly accumulate more. Some will be soft and warm, others will be energetic and exciting, or hard and cold, tiny and barely noticeable or huge and overwhelming. There will be ones that you resent, but others that you will cling onto, even going forward may never fully let go of.

She says that there are animals that still follow her, but they are all but forgotten now. They seemed important, once but now are barely there.

I think of my butterflies, my little dormouse, my stoat, even the snake.

Jayne squeezes my hand and tells me that although my cow was intimidating, there was great comfort in knowing that something like that could be created by me.

Polythrenody

As our food arrives, so does an epiphany.

I say to her that I have to find my cow, and she nods firmly.

We leave the food and call a taxi. I find myself awed by her. I have this sense that because her relationships have been so short, and perhaps numerous, that she feels intimidated by longer ones. Yet, she has a wisdom and emotional intelligence that I had never acquired, throughout all my dalliances, long or short.

I say to her as we wait for the taxi, that I have no idea where to start looking.

Jayne smiles and says that my cow will be where it grew up.

The taxi comes and we sit in silence on the way, but she holds my hand. I feel safe with her, but in a different way than I did with Pattie, and even in my long marriage to Louise.

I find myself thinking about what our animal would be. I also hope that I might not ever find out.

We arrive at Louise house and can immediately her shouting and crashing from inside. Louise is screaming yet my son is laughing his little head off.

Jayne and I head up to the front door. I push it open

and can see shapes moving in the kitchen. There is the relentless barking of the sea-lion, clearly amused by something, my sons giggling and Louise yelling furiously.

I enter first. My cow is there, still battered and bloody, and I feel a tidal wave of guilt. I did that. I should not have. For any reason.

Regardless of its wounds, the cow is walking around the kitchen table, knocking chairs over and sending dinner plates crashing to the floor. Louise is trying to push the cow away and pick broken crockery and food up.

She senses me, looks at me with a fury that is absolute and tells me in no uncertain terms, *to get this fucking thing out of her house.*

Louise's eyes drift past me to Jayne and they say hello quickly. Louise throws her hands up as the cow knocks over another chair, this one hitting a vase that smashes on the wall, soil and ceramic shards scattering everywhere.

She pushes past me, shaking her head and saying something to Jayne. I am aware that they converse, Louise about me and my failings, Jayne not agreeing, not wholly disagreeing either.

I, however, am focussed on the cow.

Polythrenody

As it turns, wedged between the wall and the dining table, it sees me and stops dead. It's dark eyes roll and fix on me.

I hold out my hand, move towards it slowly. As I do, I study the wounds that I have caused. Some are light and will heal quickly, others are deep and painful, and may never fully heal. I can treat them, but they will leave a scar that will never completely fade.

The cow's nostrils twitch as my hand draws closer, but it's doesn't jerk away as I rest my palm on its damp snout.

I hate to admit it, but I missed it. Just a little.

Louise and Jayne talk, my son still laughs at the mess and the sea-lion claps in shrill hysterics. The cow's hot, wet tongue snakes out and licks my hand gently.

It's fucking gross, but I'll get used to it.

Polythrenody

AFTERWORD

This is a collection a short stories written throughout 2020 and into '21, not initially intended as a response to the insanity of the world, but to keep myself motivated. In truth, some tales did become more than a little reactionary. Some were stories that I wanted to tell that weren't long enough for novels, others, such as *Yellow After Dark*, were adapted from short film screenplays that failed to get into production.

I decide to organise the various pieces into an anthology around the new year, working to completing the final two stories, *The Sandwich* and *Cow*, both of which are clearly largely metaphoric. Along with *Cafe Dexter*, are all allegorical pieces designed to look at important things from a different perspective, trying to trivialise the issues in order to put across how deeply important they truly are.

The Dark is a tumble of thoughts based on little tidbits

from conversations I had with various people struggling through the deepest part of the UK's Lockdown #1, pertaining to a sudden loss of direction and purpose.

Toothbrush and Pant, I won't was just a short story brief from a website that I simply had fun with and stretched beyond all reason into the bizarre tale it became. Between you and men, I feel I could do more with it. Would anyone actually want me to, is another matter entirely!

I hope you enjoyed *Polythrenody*, and please look out for my other works.

Seriously.

I need the cash.

Nick Archer

OTHER WORKS BY
NICK ARCHER

Novels
Available on Amazon

Epithalamium
A Kiss at Midnight
Carmine Grove
Drop Safe

Haiku-Noir
The Songs of our Children

COMING SOON

The Projectionist

Polythrenody

Nick Archer

Printed in Great Britain
by Amazon

79391207R00068